SIDE-SPLITTING STORIES

Michael Dahl Presents is published by Stone Arch Books,
Raintree is an imprint of Capstone Global Library Limited, a company
incorporated in England and Wales having its registered office at 264 Banbury
Road, Oxford, OX2 7DY – Registered company number: 6695582

www.raintree.co.uk
myorders@raintree.co.uk

Designed by Hilary Wacholz
Original illustrations © Capstone Global Library Limited 2021
Production by Katy LaVigne
Originated by Capstone Global Library Ltd
Printed and bound in India

ISBN: 978 1 4747 9457 2

British Library Cataloguing in Publication Data
A full catalogue record for this book is available from the British Library.

ATTACK OF THE NIGHTMARE NAPPIES

By Megan Atwood
Illustrated by Ethen Beavers

raintree
a Capstone company — publishers for children

CONTENTS

A "LAFFY" LAUGH!

Do you have funny friends? Some friends sound so goofy when they laugh that it makes others laugh too. Some people are great at telling jokes and hilarious stories. Maybe you are too. Maybe you could write down your funny ideas, jokes and stories. If you feel a chuckle or a guffaw deep inside while reading this book, just let it out!

CHAPTER 1

A NEW NEIGHBOUR IS ALL THE BUZZ

Angie DelMar held the curtain and stared out
of the window at the older woman moving in next
door. She'd hoped it would be someone who
was ten – her age – or around that age, anyway.
Instead, it looked like her new neighbour was a
boring grown-up. Summer would be a snoozefest.

Her best friend, Cooper Sanchez, droned on as
she looked. "But anyway, the nursery people said

that Chloe and Cara are two now, so they need to stop taking off their nappies. . . ."

Angie nodded but then squinted harder as she gazed out of the window. Her curly red hair got in her face, so she brushed it aside. She whistled through the gap in her two front teeth.

". . . because people have *stepped* on the nappies and got poo—"

"Cooper," Angie said, "what does that box say?"

Cooper climbed up on the couch next to her. "It says, *DO NOT TOUCH – DANGEROUS,*" he said. "Did you hear anything I just said?"

Angie nodded. "Yeah. Nappies. Nursery. Twin sisters. I got it." She flipped around and put her tongue between her teeth. "I think there's something weird about our new neighbour."

Cooper sighed. "You never listen to me."

"Huh? Did you say something? Never mind: let's go and meet our new neighbour," Angie said. She grinned her biggest grin – the one she thought could talk Cooper into anything. They'd been best friends and neighbours since they were babies. She'd learned all the tricks to trick him – or rather, *encourage* him – into doing things with her.

"Uh . . . let's wait until she's finished moving in. And until our parents make us," Cooper said, frowning.

"Let's be proactive," she said. It was her mum's favourite word. She didn't know exactly what it meant, only that her mum said it to her team when she wanted them to do something they didn't want to do. As police chief in the town, Angie's mum got to tell people what to do a lot. Angie liked doing that too.

Cooper frowned deeper. "I really don't think —"

"Great! Let's go!" Angie said. She grabbed Cooper by the hand, dragging him out the door.

They ran across the street, Angie huffing just a little. The woman had disappeared inside the house, though the door was open as removal people kept moving boxes.

When they reached the door, Cooper tugged at Angie. "Let's go back."

But Angie wasn't listening. She peered into the house and saw a door all the way at the back. A sign read, *MOVERS, DO NOT COME IN HERE UNDER ANY CIRCUMSTANCES.*

A mystery. She grinned and elbowed Cooper. "Look at that door," she whispered.

Cooper stood on his toes, and then his eyes widened. "Don't even think —"

"You're right! We should check it out!" Angie said. A removals man was coming up the front stairs. Angie got out of the way and then followed him into the house.

The mover turned to go up the stairs, and Angie walked to the mysterious door. She put her ear next to it. A strange buzzing sound came through. She turned around to wave Cooper in but stopped short.

Her new neighbour stood right in front of her. "What are you doing, girlie?" said the woman. She smiled the creepiest smile Angie had ever seen.

Angie swallowed. "We . . . uh . . . I came to meet you! I'm your neighbour," she said.

The woman frowned. "Kids, huh?" She cringed a little. She took Angie's upper arm and walked her to the front door. "You should stay out of people's houses, little lady," she said.

Cooper stood by the front door, eyes still wide. "H-hello," he said. "I'm Cooper. This is Angie."

The woman eyed him. "Another kid? This town is crawling with them," she said under her breath. "Well, I'm Ms Poodon."

Angie felt her eyes widen, and she laughed. "Ha! Ms Poodon!" But the expression on the woman's face made Angie stop laughing. She swallowed. "Oh. You weren't kidding."

"No, I wasn't, girlie. My name is Ms Poodon" – Angie couldn't help laughing again – "and this is my house you're trespassing in." She pushed Angie out of the door so she was standing by Cooper.

Cooper pointed to the book in Ms Poodon's hand. "I like to read too. What is it you're reading?"

Angie squinted to see the title. Ms Poodon hugged the book closer to her and said, "None of your business, little man. Now, time to go home." Then she shut the door in their faces.

They turned around and started walking slowly down the front steps. Cooper whispered, "Did you see the title of that book?"

Angie nodded. "Oh yeah. And I think we had better get into that secret room. Anyone who carries around a book called *ABCs of World Domination* is up to no good!"

CHAPTER 2

SNEAK-A-BOO

"It's just . . . I *know* my yoghurt would be
perfect for the nursery," Cooper's mum said.
She sat beside Angie's mum on the living room
sofa. "Kids love the stuff! And you know, the
nursery is a national chain. But Mika, Chloe and
Cara's nursery carer won't sit down with me.
And I made *so* much yoghurt, Beth. So much. It's
just sitting in a fridge in my garage." She threw

her hands up. "But she won't talk with me about it. I think she thinks I'm a fool."

Angie loved it when Cooper's mum came over to talk to hers. They got wrapped up in conversation for *hours*. Angie had no idea what the yoghurt talk was about, but she wasn't really listening. She was plotting a way to get back into Ms Poodon's house.

She shouted to her mum in one long string of words, "We're going out to play and Genevieve is meeting us!"

Her mum shouted back, "Okay, stay close!" Then she kept on talking to Cooper's mum.

Cooper followed Angie outside and crossed his arms. "You asked Genevieve to come over?" Genevieve was their mutual friend. Kind of. She was really more Angie's friend.

Angie ignored him.

Cooper said, "Did you invite Genevieve over so it would be two against one?" Just as he said that, their other, older neighbour Harvey walked up. Harvey was two years ahead of Angie and Cooper, but he still liked to hang out with them. Angie thought he was annoying. But Cooper always made her be nice.

"What are you up to this fine day?" Harvey asked. Angie rolled her eyes, and Cooper elbowed her. Harvey always sounded like he was a million years old when he spoke.

"Nothing –" Angie said.

"Want to play?" Cooper said at the same time.

Harvey said, "I'm too old to 'play' but I will spend time with you, if you so wish."

Genevieve walked up. "Hi, guys. Hi, Harvey! What's up? You said there was an emergency, Angie. I'm here!"

Cooper glared at Angie, but she pretended she didn't see. "Our new neighbour is trying to take over the world," she said. "We need to get into her house."

Genevieve blinked twice. Then, in her cheery way, she said, "Okay!"

Cooper huffed and Harvey said, "I highly doubt that an adult would –"

"I have an idea," Angie said, ignoring everyone. She pointed to some water pistols sitting in a pile on the boundary between her and her neighbour's gardens. "Harvey and Genevieve, you play water pistols and distract Ms Poodon –"

Genevieve snorted. Loud. "Did you say Ms Poodon?"

Cooper and Angie sniggered. "Yeah," Angie said.

Harvey looked at them. "Ms Poodon?"

"Yep," Angie said. "Ms Poodon." All of them giggled. Then Angie continued, "So you and Harvey will distract Ms Poodon" – they all giggled again – "while Cooper and I look in the window where the secret room is."

"I don't like it," said Cooper.

"Fun!" said Genevieve.

"Great! Let's go. I think Ms Poodon" – everyone giggled – "is in her garden. Coop and I will run around to the window while you guys squirt at each other near her. She'll shout at you – she hates kids."

Cooper said, "Wait – "

"Okay, go!" Angie said. Genevieve and Harvey ran to the squirt guns. Angie grabbed Cooper's hand and dragged him to the back window.

When they reached the window, they ducked down underneath it. Then they both slowly stood up to look through it.

But to Angie's disappointment, the blinds to the window were drawn. She kicked herself for not thinking of that.

Cooper said, huffing, "If you would *listen* to me, Angie, I would have said she probably had the blinds closed!"

Just then she heard a garbled yell. Genevieve and Harvey ran around the house. Gen was grinning madly but Harvey looked confused. "Why did you squirt that lady, Genevieve?" he asked.

"Yes, why, Genevieve?" drawled Ms Poodon. She stood there, her hair dripping. She saw Angie and Cooper, and her eyes narrowed. "YOU," she said. "Here you are again, trespassing!"

Angie stood taller. "What do you have in that secret room?" she said, sticking her chin up.

Ms Poodon grinned a not-nice grin. She took out her phone, dialled a number, and spoke into it. "Yes, police. I have some little trespassers here I'd like removed. I'm at 219 Leahy Street. I believe the trespassers' names are Cooper and Angie?"

Angie groaned. Cooper sagged next to her. And in less than a second, she heard her mum bellow, "ANGIE ROBERTA DELMAR, GET OVER HERE!" She looked slowly towards her house and saw her mum and Cooper's mum standing at the front door, hands on their hips.

Angie turned to confront Ms Poodon but she was gone. She heard a swift *shhuuush* and saw movement in the window. Ms Poodon had opened the blinds and now waved at them gleefully. She turned to the side and swept her arm around the room.

There was nothing there. A desk, a lamp and a laptop were the only things in the room. It was empty.

Cooper glared at Angie and stomped away towards his mum. Angie turned away from Ms Poodon's mean grin and walked slowly back to her own house.

Genevieve ran up to her and put her arm through Angie's. "It was worth a shot, Angie. Should I text you later?"

Angie sighed. "Yeah, that would be great. But I won't be allowed out for a few days. I'm definitely grounded."

Genevieve nodded and gave her one more squeeze then skipped away. Angie didn't even know where Harvey went.

When Angie reached her mum, Cooper was already being led away by his mum. He gave her one last look before reaching his own house next door. Angie's mum gave her a hard stare.

"What were you doing, Angie?" she asked.

"I thought that the neighbour was up to something," Angie mumbled.

Her mum sighed. "Well, did you find anything? Was it worth the two days you'll be grounded?"

Angie looked down. "Nothing. There was nothing in that room." She sighed and thought, *It's going to be a boring summer after all.*

CHAPTER 3

THE BIG IDEA

That night, Angie heard vehicles outside and that strange buzzing sound came back. Angie could not figure out where it was coming from. So strange.

When she looked out of the window, she saw a light glowing in the secret room and movement near the back door of Ms Poodon's house. Several people kept going in and out through the door.

She checked the time – three o'clock in the morning. This was definitely suspicious. Angie smiled to herself. Something was up after all.

After two long days of being grounded, Angie texted Cooper, Genevieve and even Harvey to meet her at her house. They gathered in her garden, and Angie bounced up and down.

"Ms Poodon" – they all giggled – "was up to something every single night while I was grounded. We have to get *into* that room," Angie said. She felt a pang of guilt. Her mum would be so cross with her. But if she was going to save the world, she couldn't worry about what her mum thought.

Cooper stared at her. Finally he said, "Are you kidding, Angie? There was nothing in there!"

Angie crossed her arms. "I think there is. We're just missing it somehow."

Cooper huffed. "You don't listen to anyone, Angie. I'm out of here," he said. Then he walked off.

Angie couldn't believe it. Cooper never abandoned her. Never. She sputtered for a moment then took a deep breath, watching him walk away.

Genevieve gave her a sympathetic look. Harvey looked uncomfortable.

"There may be nothing in there, but I think we have to see for ourselves," Angie said. Without Cooper, though, she wasn't so sure.

Harvey said, "There was something in there, though. A laptop."

Angie blinked. Of course. If you wanted to take over the world, you'd probably plan it on a computer. She looked at Genevieve, who was already grinning. Genevieve was a whizz at computers.

"What's the plan?" Genevieve asked. Angie could have hugged her.

"Harvey, you ring the doorbell and distract Ms Poodon." After they all stopped giggling, she finished. "Get her away from the front door so we can slip in."

Harvey shifted on his feet. "Um . . . I'm not sure I'm the best person for this job. My mum says my social skills are one rung below a wolf child's."

Angie ignored him. "Let's go." She'd show Cooper she was right. She marched towards the house. Genevieve and Harvey had no choice but to follow her.

Angie and Genevieve hid by the side of the house and Harvey rang the bell. When Ms Poodon answered, Harvey said, "Um, hi. I dropped my, uh . . . science experiment in your garden. Can you help me find it?"

Angie shook her head. Science experiment? But she heard Ms Poodon huff and watched as she walked away from the door with Harvey.

Ms Poodon complained loudly, "Children again! Today is a terrible day for this."

Angie and Genevieve sneaked in. They got into the room with no problems, though the buzzing sound had gone away. Genevieve opened the laptop and got to work.

Angie leaned over the computer as Genevieve clicked around. Soon, she found a folder that said *World Domination Plan*. Genevieve clicked on it.

"Wow, she wasn't worried about people getting into her computer," Genevieve whispered. The folder opened up.

Angie's breath caught in her throat. She had been right! Ms Poodon was planning on taking over the world.

And from what they found in the file, it seemed she was planning on doing it *today*.

Genevieve breathed out. She read, "Step one: Train insects. Check. Step two: Make growth serum. Check. Step three: Give serum to insects. Step four: Rule the world."

Angie saw a map of the room they were standing in. On it, an arrow pointed to the window they had tried to look in. Then there was a diagram of a secret drawer in the window frame on the inside. The serum, it seemed, was hidden in the woodwork around the window.

"It looks like the last two steps still haven't been done. Thank goodness. We need to steal the growth serum so she can't give it to the insects!" Angie said, her heart beating fast. "And then we gotta get out of here!"

But a voice from the doorway stopped her from moving.

"Not so fast, girlies." Ms Poodon pushed Harvey into the room with them. "Looks like I'll get to try out my plan on *three* foolish little children before it goes global."

CHAPTER 4

KICKING THE HORNET'S NEST

Ms Poodon stared at them.

"We know your plan," Angie said. She stepped in front of Genevieve and Harvey. "You are not going to get away with this!"

Ms Poodon laughed an evil laugh. "Oh yeah? Let's see what my babies have to say about this." She put two fingers in her mouth and whistled. With that, the buzzing sound came back.

Before Angie knew it, a swarm of insects flew to Ms Poodon and hovered around her head. There were wasps and hornets and other flying insects that looked terrifying. Angie screamed, horrified.

"I don't need growth serum to take care of a few measly kids," Ms Poodon said. "I just have to whistle my attack whistle and you are all toast. Any last words?" She grinned. "Wait, never mind. I don't care." Then she put her fingers in her mouth and took a deep breath. Angie squeezed her eyes shut and leaned into Genevieve and Harvey. She hadn't thought this would be her last day on earth. She was glad Cooper wasn't there – at least he would survive.

But just then, the doorbell rang.

Ms Poodon put her fingers down. "That must be my insect food. I have to feed my babies before they take over the world." She looked at Angie, Harvey and Genevieve. "Not a sound, you hear?

If you are good, maybe I'll keep you around to do work for me. Get in that cupboard."

At first, Angie stood her ground.

Ms Poodon said, "I could get them to attack you right now, you know." She put her fingers in her mouth again to whistle, but Angie put her hands up.

"Okay, okay!" she said. She, Harvey and Genevieve crowded into the cupboard. Ms Poodon loomed large over them for a second, the insects still buzzing by her head.

"I'll deal with you later," she said and shut the door. Then she opened it again. "Wait. You probably have phones. Give them to me."

The doorbell rang again, and Ms Poodon huffed. "No one has any patience any more." Angie reluctantly handed Ms Poodon her phone, and Genevieve and Harvey handed over theirs.

Genevieve said, "If I don't check in every hour, my mum comes looking for me. And you don't want my mum to find you."

Ms Poodon laughed. "Silly child. Your mum will have other things on her mind in an hour." Then she shut the cupboard door and turned the key in the lock.

They were stuck.

They heard Ms Poodon walk away, and Angie tried the door handle. It was no use. "I don't . . . have a plan," Angie said. Genevieve and Harvey were quiet. Angie felt close to tears. She was letting her friends down. Not to mention the world! Surely she could think of something. . . .

But before she could come up with anything, she heard some shuffling outside the cupboard. "Is she back already?" Genevieve whispered.

Angie steeled her shoulders. "When she opens

that door, let's all run at her. Maybe that will buy us some time."

Harvey and Genevieve nodded.

The key in the lock jiggled. Angie got ready to pounce. The door flung open, and the trio all roared and tumbled out of the cupboard at Ms Poodon. They landed in a pile on the floor.

Only it wasn't Ms Poodon. It was Cooper.

"Coop!" Angie yelled as they all climbed off him.

Cooper said, "Shhh! We don't have much time." He groaned and got up. "We have to get out of here. I overheard everything she said. We need to tell your mum, Angie!"

"We need to get that serum," Angie said, walking to the window. She felt all around the edges.

"Angie!" Cooper said. "Come on!"

Harvey and Genevieve had already moved to the window and climbed out. Cooper climbed out too, then gestured frantically for Angie to hurry up.

Sweat had started to bead up on her forehead when she found a soft spot in the wood. She pushed it in, and a drawer slid out. In it sat a skinny tube filled with bright pink liquid. Angie grabbed it, but at the same time, the door to the room flung open.

Ms Poodon stood in the doorway, the light behind her bright, the insects around her head buzzing angrily. She put her fingers to her lips, just as Angie threw one leg over the window ledge to climb out.

But it was too late. Ms Poodon whistled and yelled, "ATTACK!"

CHAPTER 5

TODDLER-TASTROPHE

The insects swarmed at them, but Cooper slammed the window just as Angie got her leg out.

"RUN!" Angie shouted and took off. Harvey, Genevieve and Cooper passed her pretty quickly. They ran through gardens, jumped over bushes, rocks, fences and anything else that got in their way.

Angie could hear the swarm of angry insects right behind her. She even felt one brush her ear and she swatted it away.

But she was running out of steam. They needed a place to hide – and fast.

They ran all through the streets towards the centre of their small town.

Angie felt close to dropping. Her lungs burned and she was starting to get a stitch.

Luckily, Cooper yelled, "This way!" and swerved into an alley.

The others followed him. To Angie's sheer joy, a door opened in one of the buildings along the alley. Cooper didn't even stop to explain to the surprised adult who had opened the door. He swept past her, followed by Genevieve and Harvey.

Angie puffed her way to the door and saw the adult's eyes widen as she caught a glimpse of the swarm of insects following closely behind.

Angie raced in, and the adult closed the door one second before the insects followed.

"What the heck was that?" the adult said.

Angie bent down and put her hands on her knees, trying to catch her breath. She wasn't the only one. Cooper, Genevieve and Harvey were also bent over and breathing hard.

The adult shook her head. "Well, I guess we won't take the kids out to the playground today," she said.

Angie stood up and looked around. They were in a large playroom that was empty. She heard yelling from little voices in a room next door.

"Where are we?" she said, still panting.

Cooper looked around too and then grinned. "We're at my sisters' nursery! Hi, Mika!" he said to the adult.

She smiled at Cooper. "Hi, Cooper. I didn't recognize you in all the chase. So nice to see you. I bet Chloe and Cara would love to see you too."

"This is Mika," Cooper said to Angie, Genevieve and Harvey. "She's the nursery owner here. She looks after my sisters."

Angie widened her eyes. "That's great, Coop. But we need to use the phone right now."

Cooper narrowed his eyes. "We have the serum, Angie. We're out of danger," he said quietly.

"I have to get back to the room," Mika said. "Come and say hi to your sisters, Cooper!"

"We don't have time —" Angie said.

At the same time, Cooper said, "Yes!" He started walking to the door at the other end of the room.

Angie caught up with him. She held out the serum. "We have to get this somewhere safe, Cooper!"

"We will," he whispered. "We can ask to use the phone once we're in here."

Angie sulked as they stepped into the room.

It was pure chaos. Toddlers ran around everywhere. Nappies were strewn all around the room. Toys cluttered every surface. Some kids were crying, some were laughing. Some fought in the corner and some just ran around in circles.

Cooper looked down at the serum and took it from Angie.

She tried to pull it back, but Cooper said, "Just

let me look at it." They wrestled with it back and forth, Genevieve and Harvey sharing a look.

"COOPER!" yelled two small voices through the racket of all the other toddler noises. A tangled mess of plaits and little arms and legs flew at them. Cooper and Angie were enveloped in big hugs from Chloe and Cara.

The twins pulled away and then ran back to the middle of the room. After she regained her balance, Angie watched as the twins stood close together with their backs to her. They were looking at something. Other toddlers began to crowd around them.

Angie looked down at her hands. She looked at Cooper's hands.

Their hands were empty.

Cooper and Angie looked at each other and said, "Oh no," at the same time.

Just then, Angie heard the sound of glass hitting the floor. A pink waft of serum enveloped the group of toddlers.

Angie watched in horror as the toddlers began to grow.

And grow . . . and grow . . . and grow . . .

Until their heads knocked into the ceiling and then pushed the ceiling clean off the building.

CHAPTER 6

GIANT TODDLER ALERT!

The giant toddlers stepped out of the building.

Angie and Cooper stared at each other in horror. "Now what do we do?" Genevieve asked across the room.

At least ten toddlers were now as big as tall, tall buildings. They toddled off through the town. Angie, Cooper, Harvey and Genevieve tried to follow them.

Cooper said, "I just hope my sisters don't —"

But then Angie saw what he was afraid of. Chloe and Cara looked at each other and giggled.

Then they unhitched their nappies and let them drop.

The four friends raced to get out of the way of the sloppy nappies, which were now as big as three buildings side by side. With a huge *THWUMP*, the nappies landed. To Angie's horror, the contents spilled out of them and splatted on the buildings and on the street. She barely managed to jump out of the way of the splat.

Worse, the other toddlers saw the twins take off their nappies. One by one, each toddler took off theirs.

Angie, Cooper, Genevieve and Harvey started running. At each step, they were almost flattened

by gigantic soiled nappies. Just as they turned one way, another toddler was taking off a nappy. As they ran away from that toddler, they ran towards another one who thought it was funny to drop his nappy.

THWUMP THWUMP THWUMP.

SPLATTTTT.

The town was now draped in dirty nappies. There was poo *everywhere*.

The toddlers started to play. They picked up cars and *vroooomed* them on the streets. One toddler grabbed a helicopter out of the sky and put it down on top of one of the buildings.

But Chloe and Cara were the worst of the bunch. Each of them had poo in their hands, and they decided to throw it at each other and the other toddlers.

SPLAT.

SPLAT.

SPLATTTT.

The sound of the poo hitting things was almost as bad as the smell.

"Watch out!" yelled Cooper as a big pile of poo came tumbling down, almost on Angie's head. It didn't matter though. Anyone who was anywhere near the toddlers had poo all over them.

Adults lined the streets, yelling to the toddlers, "DO YOU WANT A TIME-OUT?" But the little ones weren't listening. One of the toddlers started to cry. Huge, deadly drops of tears began to land hard on the ground. Everyone on the street scattered.

Angie looked at her friends. "Now what?"

CHAPTER 7

GO 'GURT 'EM!

Genevieve said, "On the computer, I saw that there's an antidote in Ms Poodon's house! It's under a floorboard below the window."

Angie said, "Well, that's something. Let's go! We can work out what to do when we get there."

They ran as fast as they could back to their neighbourhood. They could hear the thumps of giant toddler feet behind them.

When they reached Ms Poodon's house, they found her sitting outside in her garden, her legs splayed out and her chin on her fist. A confused looking swarm of insects surrounded her. The four of them slowed down and tried to sneak past her. But when they reached her door, she looked up.

"HEY! You kids ruined EVERYTHING! I hate children." She whistled, and the insects snapped into shape, swarming around her head. "You'll pay for this!"

She took a deep breath in to shout, but a big shadow blotted out the sun. She looked up and said, "What the heck?"

Chloe stood looking down at her, her face a little red and straining.

"Uh-oh, I know that look!" said Cooper. "Get inside!"

The four of them rushed into the house and shut the door. They heard a giant *SPLAT* and the windows got splattered with a huge pile of . . . poo.

Angie gagged. "I almost feel sorry for her!" she said.

"There's no time!" said Genevieve. While they'd watched Ms Poodon get splatted on, she'd run into the room and grabbed the antidote. "I have the cure. But how do we get it to the toddlers?"

They all looked at Angie expectantly. But she did something she never did. Maybe because she and Cooper had had an argument and she'd got everyone in this mess. Or maybe because she remembered that Cooper was super clever and always had great ideas – whether she listened or not. Or maybe it was because she was covered in poo. But whatever the reason, she said, "Let's see if Cooper has any ideas."

Cooper smiled at her. He took a minute to think. Then his face lit up. "Yoghurt! My mum had tons of it in our garage."

Angie whooped. "That's a perfect idea!" she yelled. She beamed at Cooper. "You know, sometimes you have some good things to say." Cooper smiled back at her.

Harvey said, "But how do we get them to eat it?"

Angie and Cooper looked at each other and grinned. "WATER PISTOLS!" they said at the exact same time.

CHAPTER 8

MS POODON IS DONE

The four of them grabbed the water pistols and filled them with Cooper's mum's yoghurt. Angie tasted it just to be sure. It really was delicious. They added drops of the antidote to each water pistol.

Then they ran outside and squirted their first toddler – Chloe. She licked her lips and instantly shrunk down to her normal toddler size. She immediately started to cry.

Cooper's mum came out of her house and grabbed Chloe. She saw Cooper and said, "What is going on?" Then she pinched her nose.

Cooper yelled, "Be back in a sec, Mum!"

Angie yelled, "Your yoghurt is delicious, Ms Sanchez!"

Then the four of them sprinted to the town, dodging poo and other unpleasant things, to shoot some toddlers with yoghurt.

One by one, each toddler shrank down to toddler size. Adults grabbed the toddlers as they went back to normal. Soon, the nursery was filled with crying, dirty, smelly, tired toddlers.

Angie, Cooper, Genevieve and Harvey walked back to Angie's house. They had poo smeared everywhere, and Angie had never been so tired in her life. But she felt great. Not only had they saved

the world, but the summer *definitely* wasn't boring so far.

When they got back to Angie's house, they saw Ms Poodon – covered in poo – loading up her car.

"YOU AGAIN!" she yelled. "My babies are gone, and now I have nothing! But no problem, I'll just try again in the next town."

Angie sighed. Really, she was too tired for this. "Do you guys have any ideas on how to stop her?"

Cooper grinned. "I like this new thing of you listening to other people."

Angie grinned back.

Just then, a siren sounded near them. Angie's mum pulled up in a police car. "Ms Poodon," she said – the kids all giggled. Angie thought her mum might have even sniggered a little. "You are under arrest!"

Angie was thrilled. "Mum! How did you know she was behind this?"

As her mum put handcuffs on Ms Poodon, she said, "You know I *do* listen to you. I talked to Mika at the nursery, and I worked out that Ms Poodon" – everyone giggled, Angie's mum included – "was behind this. You're my daughter – your instincts are pretty good," she said and smiled.

Angie's mum put Ms Poodon in the back seat then walked to the driver's side door. "Oh, and Cooper, good news! The nursery has decided to buy your mum's yoghurt. It really is delicious." She shut her door and said, "All right, Angie, I'll see you later tonight. I have some cleaning up to do." She turned on the sirens and drove away.

Ms Poodon glared at all four of them out of the back window for as long as she could before the car disappeared down the street.

Cooper threw his arm around Angie and she threw her arm around Genevieve, who threw her arm around Harvey.

"Well, that was an interesting start to our summer," Cooper said.

Angie smiled. "I can't wait to see what else happens! Didn't you think that the nursery seemed haunted or something? We should probably do some investigating. . . ."

All of them groaned, but Angie couldn't stop smiling.

GLOSSARY

antidote a medicine to cure a poison

bellow to shout very loudly

circumstances facts or conditions that are connected to an event

drawl to speak in a slow manner

gleefully in a very joyful manner

proactive to make something happen instead of reacting to something

serum a liquid that is used to prevent or cure a disease

sympathetic expressing feelings of pity or sadness for someone else who's going through something hard

toddle to move with short, unsteady steps

trespass to go onto someone's property without permission

DISCUSSION QUESTIONS

1. How did Angie change over the course of the story? How did she stay the same?

2. Throughout the book, Cooper seems frustrated about Angie not listening to him. If you had a friend like Angie, how would you let her know that you want her to listen to you?

3. If Angie and her friends hadn't found an antidote, what else do you think the toddlers might have got up to?

WRITING PROMPTS

1. What investigation do you think Angie and her friends will take on next? Write your own funny story about the friends' next adventure.

2. Imagine you're a news reporter in Angie's town. Write an article about what happened with Ms Poodon, the toddlers and Angie and friends.

3. What was Ms Poodon thinking when she planned to unleash giant insects in her neighbourhood? Write a paragraph or two from her perspective. How does she feel about her plans being ruined by the neighbourhood kids?

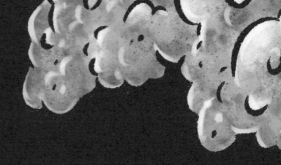

ABOUT THE AUTHOR

MEGAN ATWOOD is a writer and professor with more than 45 books published. She lives in New Jersey, USA, where she wrangles cats, dreams up ridiculous stories and thinks of ways to make kids laugh all day.

ABOUT THE ILLUSTRATOR

ETHEN BEAVERS has been working in children's books, comics and animation for more than 10 years. He is a big fan of Star Wars and Samurai Jack, as well as fly-fishing for trout.

JOKING AROUND

How do you get a baby astronaut to sleep?
You rocket!

Why did the coach hire a baby for his team?
Because it's so good at dribbling!

Why did the cowboy give cough syrup to the pony?
It was a little hoarse!

What did the burger name its baby?
Patty!

What do they call babies in the army?
Infantry!

What do you get if you cross a baby with a mountain?
A cry for Alp!

What do you find on the bottom of a baby cloud?
Thunderwear!

READ MORE
SILLY STORIES!

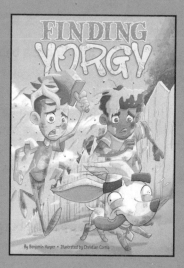

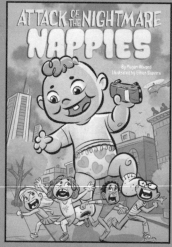